WAKE UP BEFORE YOU REGRET

AN EXPOSURE TO THE PRACTICAL WORLD

WAFIYA FAIZ

FOR

All those who accept me as I am

Contents

Contents

Prologue

Life is a series of events. We all come across trouble and sorrow. Grieving upon regrets can only suffer our bodies. The real wisdom lies in the fact to accept the loss without letting grief overcome or defeat us. Life was normal before Radhika faced the biggest challenge. She soon was introduced to the angel of her life that changed the very course of her life but not everyone is as grateful as she. Every soul has to taste loss. Some people see the world through the filter of optimism and some do not. If your life is miserable then you are miserable to others too. The person with a negative attitude dwells on problems and one with a positive one concentrates on solutions. It is important to see possibilities rather than excruciating limitations.

If you find possibilities before regretting them then it is a fortunate gift for you.

Inconvertible situations of worldly pleasure
Caged with the urban dreams,
Pell-mell pace of materialistic satiation,
We are all stuck with the mundane contemplation
Of future events, pertaining to every
Resistance of prognosticating.
We all are immure in the musings
Of undignified contentment of immortal soul.
Hoping yet to emancipate
Hoping yet to fly again.

we all grow through what we go through.

1

Life is a series of event

Every one of us has a different notion of life. For some, it is full of joy and for many, it is a sorrowful event. However, it is only our creation of the mind that makes it complicated. Sometimes it feels like our life is over and there is no other option to move on the easiest way of getting rid of this problem is suicide which gives salvation to all problems and chaos in life but is this the only solution to overcome your problem? The answer is absolutely not. One may think that his life is most deteriorated than others without knowing others' life problems. This is a common perception that kills our morals every day. Our problem will become a piece of cake from the day we start understanding others' misery. Life isn't easy or hard to live. It is a series of events that one has to understand to overcome his problem. It is popularly said that every cloud has a silver lining, similarly, every sorrowful event is followed by a period of joy and happiness. If today is tough and hard to survive, tomorrow it will be memorable to live.

Blaming others or yourself for the thing that had already happened can give nothing more than grief. So it is better to learn from the past and move on because you grow with what you go through. It is inevitable that these immotile things also get aged with time same as we humans. Thus they grow each day with time and that too twice. One with the rhythm of life and the other with memories of mankind. There are moments when words like failure, loser, a defeated person keep taunting you and you feel like giving. If it happens today, It will end tomorrow in a more exciting and enthusiastic manner and thus creating a lifelong memory. In science, we were taught that living things respire, move, respond to stimuli and grow but it fails to define that even non-living things can also grow and have life within them. Books, furniture, clothes, paper everything grows with time and creates memories with human beings and animals.

Humans have a greater association with their home and they share incessant memories passing from one generation to other. It is inevitable that these immotile things also get aged with time same as we humans. Thus they grow each day. Is it easy to drain out fish from the ocean river and keep them alive or to fade away Diwali's lightning or shed leaves from the palm tree? These are unexpected events and parallel to these are our life's problems. Pain, grief, suffering, agony are parts of our life and we need to learn to survive with this. On the contrary love and care can heal all problems of your life.

2

Life demands Love

There is often a time when you want to achieve something concrete or a goal behind you that is extremely important to achieve. Some get achieved while some remain a dream to be accomplished. These are two common circumstances but what if your goal is abstract and not visual? At this time it becomes much tougher. Besides this, it becomes a cause for disappointment. We started losing hope and desire to work for it. Gradually it appears to be the most deteriorating element to ruin our life and here comes the power of love and care. It isn't easy to run away from our failures but to act according to the circumstances is paramount.

The definition of love varies from person to person. It is eternal in sense and has a never-ending pursuit but love cannot only be within the limits that society has fixed it so far. Love helps you to achieve your dream, it teaches you to work harder than others, it makes you feel precious and in some cases, it helps to save your life as well. Life demands love when there is a need for it. This is the same as we remember God only at the time of suffering. Everything goes good as long as we do not encounter any trouble and can manage things on our own. When things go horribly wrong we immediately turn to our love but this is not only a turning from one side. When you suffer from the toughest time of your life and one phone call or message swings your mood all of a sudden is the time you realise the importance of love and its need in life.

3

Counter your problem

At the time I started hating myself and even expected others to hate me as well. I was afraid of sharing this with anyone as it always appears to be a fictional story from 16 years old girl. All my life, I was discouraged from visiting my insight soul and I was the only one to disconsolate myself. Growing up in a happy cheerful family was a gift for me and it was never expected to hear anything that has disheartened me. It is amusing to hear from a joyous teen about life and their problems. This is a general perception of our community. The norms that they lay down and the things they tell you is paramount, despite the care that you might end up frustrated. This was the same condition for me. Our society has created certain rules for how to act whom to love and what to say.

They never care about the insight of your minds or your choice. The first step of hindrance comes from your home itself. It becomes challenging to cope with your kith and kin. Though their love is undeniable their methods are not. To overcome this hurdle is to prove to them that you were and you are right and this can be done through actions and not through arguments. They would not get you until you act wisely which cannot be ignored. Another option of healing yourself from disappointment is to do something that helps you to crystallise your thoughts. When I suffered from this chaos I prefer writing and scribbling my introspection on a piece of paper. This gives me relief at some point but later everything reappears in my mind and I feel like giving up. The reason for this can be anything - for instance, getting a low percentage of marks in an exam or miserable day or adverse thoughts or it can be anything. Love can help us at this moment. When you have people in life who can treat your big things as their big things and small happiness as their moment to joy, then you are fortunate enough to counter your problems.

For me, it is my mother and friends. It is not easy to find those people in life as it may seem to be with you but your realisation about their existence for you is unforeseen. It is also expensive to get such people, if you have them then you are the richest person on earth. You are blessed to receive the love that life demands. Your job is to save this and give equal importance before you lose it.

I'm weary with my thoughts of ending up

I'm drained to fight with battles of my head

But when I'm with you

My mania of giving up

Glide up to the sky

Hoping to live

To laugh

And to love

4

The Story Begins

Childhood is a perfect word to describe a life of fun and joy. Roaming around the street fearlessly with friends and having a lot of fun with them in the park. It is the best time to describe laughter. It is a time when we do not care about the future, money and fame or expertise. Life goes like an open ocean without any hurdles but soon like every open ocean, it also gets collided with an anonymous traveller. The only difference lies in the number of barriers. The time that comes after childhood is not easy to deal with. It follows with a fight among society, work, people and with yourself. Radhika was a middle-class girl in her late teens. Life was carried out smoothly. Hundreds of kilometres away from the bustling township, a young woman lives full of determination to achieve something big. In the whole of her life, she has never encountered any outside male of her age.

She grew up in a society where girls were not allowed to openly talk with boys. In a complete female environment, Radhika always finds herself confined and inactive. On an occasional visit to the city, She gets to know from her friends and relatives about the boys and their friendship. She was herself surprised to hear all these and always dream of having at least one date with a male company. Radhika was fortunate enough to have her cousin bhumi who accompany her whenever she visits the city. Bhumi and her friends were unlike Radhika and has travelled to different places. They gradually become good friends of Radhika too but she rarely got any chance to visit her place. It seldom happens to talk with them about any male friends as Radhika's mother always her ears up for her girl.

5

A Gift of Pleasure

On a summer visit to bhumi's house, both the sister got a chance to spend the entire day alone as their parents went out to the funeral of their neighbour. Social media has recently dominated the market and has young members more to connect with. Internet was young and so they too. Bhumi introduced this to Radhika. Fortunately, Radhika was offered an android phone with a full internet package by Bhumi as a present for her birthday. Like every other youth, this young girl too easily gets connected with the newly introduced gadget. She made an account on Facebook and the only thing that she wanted and could think about was to make friends. Time started flying on the internet and it kept her busy too. Radhika's orthodox family had not cared much about it. Their daughter did not have much to do earlier but now she at least spends her day doing something better than nothing.

Now Radhika became much familiar with social media and its uses. She spent most of her time finding friends online and so her lifestyle changed. Its been a month since she has used Facebook but had not found the courage to send friend requests to any male. Soon she thought of trying it once to send a random friend request. It was the time of the early twenties, in the era of hopeless romance neither in movies nor on benches in the park. Radhika wanted one love in her life, to console her and help her in a tough time. This was also the desire out of non-interaction of any opposite gender. Besides this, she had no friends in her town to whom she can share things. Radhika was desperate to have one person in her life with whom she can share everything -her life, her happiness, her sorrows and every other thing and she had not found anyone like that yet. It has been five days and her friend request was yet not accepted. She lost her chance of getting in touch with any such people.

What I missed to tell is that Radhika studied in an all-girls school which is nearby her village. It was nowhere any formal education. Girls there learn about regional languages, culture and sewing. Couple of years ago an educated elite of her village had taken an initiative to teach the English language to all girls of that village. This was a blessing for Radhika and even helped her to get aware of social media. She had also learnt a few English words from her cousin bhumi during her periodic visit. Her parents never care about this much as for them the ultimate goal of a female is to get married and be a good housewife, Radhika was so a good cook and advanced herself in household work. Like every other day, Radhika after her 2 hours of classes came home at a usual time and after having her lunch opened Facebook in the hope of getting in touch with someone.

6

A Little Hope of Happiness

All of a sudden Radhika burst out of happiness and the world around her turned colourful as she saw this notification on Facebook: Friend Request accepted. She immediately clicked on the notification to see who this person was, and his name appeared as Reyansh Aggarwal. There was no profile picture, no picture with friends and no cover page. She did not care much about this and opened his chatbox and sent a normal "hii". Now that Radhika's hope grew a bit and now and then she hoped to get a reply. She kept checking her phone every time but had received no message. During her bedtime, Radhika checked her phone for the last time and was startled to see a reply from Reyansh. There was a simple hello from his side. At this moment she thought nothing more and thank him for accepting her friend request. Since Radhika has been introduced to the English language, She did not find it more difficult to start the conversation following the same tongue. Their conversation continued for a while and Reyansh appeared to be much more friendly than anticipated.

He shared all her pieces of information without any hesitation and so did Radhika. He comes from the capital Delhi and is currently pursuing MBA from IILM Institute for Higher Education. In the first conversation, only Reyansh introduced himself plenty enough that nothing was left for Radhika to interrogate. He was 25 years elder than this girl. After an hour of conversation, he gave his picture to Radhika to which she glanced for a minute. She was stunned to see all this. All this astonished her as she has never spoken to any boy in her life. Reyansh was a handsome man with a charming personality. He was indeed striking and was easy to be figured out. Now it was Radhika's turn to describe herself, before that she just nodded at his chat, hardly uttering any words. After the introduction was over, he texted her 'You seem to become a good friend, I find you interesting '. This was out of the blue for her since there was not anything interesting to be appreciated but deep inside she was happy to chat with a male person for the first time.

7

Seads of Freindship

During the entire conversation. Radhika kept smiling and it was a smile that appear to be special. She was a pure-hearted girl and didn't lie about her education, she openly described all her life's scenarios and this might have captivated Reyansh. They chatted for 3 hours continuously and now with a happy note they ended up hoping to text again. For him, it may not be something exceptional but for Radhika, it was all like a dream. She finally texted a man and dared to courage to speak. Throughout the night, she only thought about her conversation with Reyansh. The Next morning, when she woke up the first thing that came to her mind was to check the phone and surprisingly there was a text by Reyansh stating "Good Morning friend".

Radhika waited for a moment and thought about this new friendship. Well after a while she texted him back the same thing. After returning from her class, she promptly checked her phone but there was no message. The entire day went out and she has received no message from his side. A Couple of days later, Reyansh messaged her and apologised for the late reply. He persuaded her that he got busy with his internship programme. They again spoke for an hour or more. This has now become a usual routine for each other. He has never asked Radhika about her picture but one day he texted his imaginative image of her in his mind. He simply wrote ' I can imagine you being an angel of heaven with a serene face and long black hair. Rosy lips and a fair outlook', this was so special for her to receive. First of all, she has never spoken to any boy and now that the first boy she talks to calls her interesting, elegant and embraces her. This was a bolt from the blue for her.

8

How would she feel?

Days passed, Months passed and so did the years. Now it becomes a habit for Radhika to talk with Reyansh. They both have shared much about each other and Rahika grew intimacy with his first-ever online friend. She shares all her events of life with Reyansh without any hesitation and for her, it all seemed like a dream. Everything was stable Radhika. Life was now filled with love and care. She expect the same feeling from Reyansh although he never expressed this his course of action was enough for Radhika to anticipate. It was a chilling summer day, with blue sky, sunshine and everything was fine. As of every day Radhika finished her household work and using her cell phone. She was waiting for Reyansh message but before that, a thunderstorm broke into her life. Radhika's parents had received a marriage proposal for her daughter from a well-to-do family and found no reluctance to accept this, without the concern for Radhika's wish. When this news approached her, it created a sudden shock in her life.

How could she marries a man who is a complete alien and to whom she never talks? She later realised that this is only written in her destiny because almost everyone in her village got married similarly but this time she took a vow to change her destiny. The reason behind accepting the marriage proposal for Radhika's parents was their financial status, their daughter's dull facial colour and it will be proud for them that their daughter get married to a rich household despite that the man is divorced and twice the age of Radhika. It was no late for her to message Reyansh and narrate the entire events. Radhika was anxious about his reaction to this but it consoles her when Reyansh showed his sympathy for her.

9

Let's stay together

That night they both speak to each other on-call which is a rare privilege for Radhika as her mother might catch her. She seemed much anxious and was sobbing throughout the conversation. Reyansh tried to comfort her but could not succeed.

"I love you, Radhika," Reyansh said softly.

There was a silence spread everywhere like a deserted island. It was an unexpected event for a village girl to get a proposal in such a manner. Radhika closed her eyes, thinking, trying to find the right words and gently she says" Reyansh, I Love you too and I want to be with you for the rest of my life."

She still cannot manage to stop her tears but it was no more tears of pain but of love and happiness. On one side Radhika was envisaging the love of her life and on the other side, her parents were busy with wedding preparation. Once the wedding date was set, time seemed to fly rapidly. Reyansh was planning one after the other to escape his lady friend from the clutches of the traditional bond. It was also a burden for Radhika's parents to get her married before she reaches 18 which is an orthodox view of countryside men and women.

10

An escape to a fairy land

Radhika was to visit her cousin Bhumi's residence before her wedding. This came as an opportunity for her to run away. She decided to add Bhumi to her plan too and after all, she is the one to help in her escape. The family reached Lucknow on Saturday night. Reyansh had already left for Lucknow and was ready with the plan. Bhumi was to take Radhika to the famous Rumi Darwaza where Reyansh was ready with his car to make her run away. It was not easy to persuade Radhika's parents but after relentless pleading they finally permitted them. Everything went according to plan. They reached the destination at 4 PM as per the decision. Reyansh was supposed to be in a black car near the gateway side. They waited for 15 minutes and after a while, a black Suzuki reached the decided spot. Reyansh was found to be inside the car. He appeared to be smarter than his picture.

11

Encounter with the reality

A young dazzling man in a slate colour shirt looks admirable. Radhika was astonished by him and so was Bhumi. Both the couple shared contact for a minute and Radhika passed a gentle smile. As she moved towards the main gate to reach out to the car, she was shocked to see that Reyansh without even a word drive his car back. A second late she called him which was rejected and did not bother to text him repeatedly. A minute later she found that she was been blocked. It was astonishing even for her. Amid the crowded road, Radhika found her alone with a broken heart. She thought about her future, her wedding and everything now deteriorated. She was left with no hope. It was the most unexpected event of her life and now she started contemplating the most genuine question "why". When it was all planned and accepted then what was the reason he left her alone. Bhumi took her to the roadside and sympathize her.

"Now it is time to go home," Bhumi said to Radhika.

They started moving but all of a sudden they saw a sudden commotion that broke out at the city's popular bakery shop. Everyone started running out of help. A massive fire broke out at a nearby shop. There was a violent rustling and shaking, as if from the thrashing of some hidden beast. The crowd lost their control and so did Radhika who was already morose. She saw herself in the middle of the crowd without her cousin and started screaming aloud. Bhumi did try to find Radhika but failed in her attempt. There was complete pandemonium, everyone just panicked.

12

Heart don't break around here

Bhumi was somehow able to rescue herself and reached home safely. The entire family member rebuked her a lot which was anticipated. Everyone put their effort to find Radhika but it was uneasy to find her in this huge city. Her parents in the grief of their only daughter's loss felt terribly sick. It was the most horrible day in their life and so were Radhika's too. After the crowd ease down, she found herself alone. she saw dead bodies around. Some corpse were covered with a white sheet, some were laid down in open. There were people who got injured and were in hurry to be treated. Radhika too was slightly injured.

She was taken to the hospital by the rescued team and her wound was treated there. Now for Radhika the biggest question was where to go? She felt secluded. She spent that night in the hospital itself. It was the biggest life lesson for her. She abandoned her parents for a stranger and trusted him more than anyone. Her wedding which was to be taken place in the coming week went in vain. Radhika was left with nothing. She broke into a cold sweat. She sat for ten minutes on the threshold of the doctor's cabin. The other patients were unaware of her inner turmoil. For nurses and staff, it was just another ordinary day but for her, it felt like the end of the world. She was sitting near the cabin of Dr Meghna, a veteran in her field. She stared at Radhika and felt like she was in help.

"what happened? Are you all right?" She asked with an anxious gesture.

Radhika was lost in her musings. She replied later which made Dr Meghna more worried about her.

"How can I find my way. I'm lost. I have destroyed everything". Radhika cried while saying these lines.

13

Hope exists everywhere

The doctor further asked about her parent's home, and where she comes from?

Did she lose her parents because of last night's chaos?

In a gloomy tone, she said

"I abandoned them. I run out of my home in the hope of better life"."

Look, little girl. Just be strong. Life is about hurdles and obstacles. You need to face it rather than grieve over". Said the doctor

For a second Radhika felt that there still some hope exists but she could not come out of her pain and simply asked

"How can I be strong after losing everything? Where will I go? Who will feed me?"

Dr Meghna without a minute late immediately took Radhika to her car and said

"Every cloud has a silver lining".

Radhika still cannot believe that she was being helped. She can now be retrieved. During their journey in a car, She narrated the entire event. Dr Meghna had spent years in London to work on curing the mental health of those who suffered from a sudden source of distress. Radhika was now her patient. She took her to the hotel where she was currently residing. She told Radhika that she will be taking her to Delhi, her home place and she was in Lucknow on an event and accidentally working in that hospital and came across her. She made her realise that this is an opportunity to work on her remedy.

It is no late to Wake Up.

Meghna came as an angel in Radhika's life. She took her to Delhi where she lives alone but now she has a companion. Finally, it was time to leave the pain aside. Radhika was on one-month treatment and as soon as her mental status was stable, Dr Meghna decided to work on her studies.

14

Why Me?

Since she did not have any professional degree nor had she completed her school properly. The initial two years were difficult for her. Dr Mrghna looked up to Radhika every time and worked on her. She treated her like a younger sister. Radhika passed her high school with good grades and was soon to be admitted to a well-reputed college. It is of no doubt that it was her strong willpower and determination alone that had bounced back her so quickly. Radhika was now done with her school. She feels calm in Meghna's company. They both share good company and now she is no more a middle village girl. In her past couple of years, she had been raised in a luxury. Dr Meghna take care that all her needs are to be fulfilled. One evening in a usual conversation with Meghna, Radhika asked the question that she always wanted to be but never got the courage to do so.

What made you spend on me? I'm like a stranger to you. You gave me another life. Why did you do this? What else do you get in return? Radhika asked.

15

Another side of the story

Dr Meghna started smiling. She looks quadruple times more beautiful while smiling.

"I saw little Meghna in you, " she said pleasantly.

Now Radhika was struck with more questions than before.

She simply said

"I want to know about this. You must have suffered something"

"There is a story. Are you certain to hear it?"

Dr Meghna asked.

Yes, Radhika confirmed.

She was eager to know and could not wait any more.

"I lived in Himachal Pradesh till I was seventeen. Daughters were not very much welcomed in my village. My mother, the most glamorous lady in this world had a dream of having a daughter and so was I born. Everyone hated me. My grandmother tried to kill me but my mother rescued me every time. I had a dream of becoming what I am today. I had a dream of travelling across the world, to bring in people's mind that girls are no less than boys".

"So how did you manage to accomplish all this?" Radhika asked.

Her eyes brighten as she continued. "I was not allowed to study until I was ten. I learnt basic things from my cousin's book. He was a boy and so was fortunate enough to go to school. When I was nine my mother run away. She was beaten several times for giving birth to a girl child. She went to her house but nobody welcomed her there. I had seen my mother crying, being thrown away by people and facing every hurdle of her life in raising me. That day I promised myself that one day I will make her proud. Finally, my mother got a job in a generous family in Solan. She did the cleaning and cooking there. The family was magnanimous. They sent me to study in school. We spent our 7 years there. I completed high school and celebrated my fifteenth birthday with fun and joy. The family treated me as their daughter. I discovered my mother's happiness. She used to live from now. It was now my time to get admitted to college and look after my future. Those days were pure and serene. Uncle Freddy introduced me to multiple scholarships and I applied to all of them. He always acknowledged me for my studies".

Dr Meghna's mind went to the happy past. She fell quiet.

Radhika was silently listening to her.

16

Patterns of Life

"I was too infatuated by a young boy of my age. We two were good friends but it soon turned out to be something different. When I got into a college in Delhi, We promised to write to each other and we did for a few months but later I found no response from him. I had visited back once during the holidays and found him to be with someone else. I realised it was not what I thought. I moved on. I completed my Medical studies in Delhi and it was a funded one which I received from a scholarship but I always thank uncle Freddy. He is a blessing to me. I was posted to Bombay as a senior doctor in the Medical field. I worked in my field and gained a reputation. I keep on visiting countries and Radhika the honorary degree which you keep staring is what I received from Bristan.

Look Radhika, Life is not like a fairy tale romance as we see in movies. It is different from what one perceives. The patterns that have shaped your life difficult need time to consolidate and it is only you who can vanish them. There is so much beauty in life. You only need to find it. In my case, it was uncle Freddy and in yours it was me. We are grateful to God for having our backbones but it is not always for others. When I first hear your story I felt like your life would be destroyed if not protected and it was only you who was to destroy your own life.

I hope you now received your answer."

Dr Meghan got up and went to her room staring at Radhika from distance.

Dr Meghna's story had created an impact. Her story had a whirlpool effect on Radhika.

She went to Meghna and asked

"What happened to that boy? Did not he regret to betray you?"

"He came to me apologising for what he did". Meghna said.

"so what did you do next? Did you give him chance?" Radhika asked as in hurry.

Dr Meghna smiled with a glow and said

"It was not love and he knows this well.

I am blessed that I woke up before I could regret it".

17

Reality is always different

Radhika finished her studies in Delhi and worked as a school teacher there.

She visited her parents and apologised for her mistakes.

She took her parents to Delhi and lived with them.

Dr Meghna got married and travelled to London.

Bhumi started work in the corporate field and keep visiting Radhika.

It remains a mystery to Radhika what reason made Reyansh leave her that day.

It was probably the beauty that she saw in filtered pictures but refused to accept the real Radhika.

Like every fairy tale story, this story could also be filled with love and romance but the reality is always different.

18

Everything happens for a reason

Life is difficult sometimes and it is only you who can deal with it. We might feel happy at one point as to achieving every goal that we set in life but eventually, there is a time when everything takes away. It becomes extremely important to deal with this situation of life when things that mean the most to you vanish. One needs to face the grief and praise it. Everything happens for a reason. Accept the trouble and find out what satiates you. If you want to make life meaningful then create a treasure of memories which keep on going. Beauty exists everywhere in life. We need to find this beauty of life. Once we find this, life will become a beautiful set of wings.

Like a set of favourite songs, we need to create a trove of commemoration that will keep us fervent.

19

The real contentment

Death has its own beauty, it's about the beauty of emotions that mankind carries throughout his life, and it's about the beauty of exploring the new world away from toxicity. Nobody is alive, we all r composed of the dead soul. Being alive only meant to move around with this worldly pleasure and one day this curse will ruin our life.

so it's better to accept the other side of life.

Consolidation of his soul

No more words to pour

Each breath was a recount

As the last wind sparked out

Not a treasure in the world saved him

Nor any victory waive him

Apprehended in his own embodiment

Anticipated by the victory of Almighty

His suffering was unbearable

His pain was intolerable

Away from the toxicity of the world

In the cold ice of heaven to be observed

Poignant on his demise

For him, it was a blessing in disguise

Two of his token left behind

His love for them was blind

Mild with the solitariness of care

All that was perceived as rare

His agony was severe

That closed his eyes forever

It was a death that keep him apart

Yet another mile to restart

Importance Of Self-observation

Over a while, I realised the importance of self-observation. It is important to hold yourself in one being. I realised how curious I become when something attracts me. It can be anything a person, place or a thing. The attraction will let us to a hypothetical world where everything surrounds us. Glorifying these moments is not wrong but merely dependent on it will get it into an unhappy life. The attraction has a similar proportionality to sadness because the day things attracted us will be the most cherishing one but after a moment it will put us into a desperate world. However, self-observation will eradicate this need for attraction. self-observation isn't only meant to turn our attention inward. It tells us the thought, emotion, and sensation that occurs within our soul. We need to go deep inside it and as we get into it, our attraction will be just for a moment. It's imperfect to change it in a day or two. Everything needs time but once it vanishes, life will become an unfolding gift of God.

Epilogue

This was a short journey through the reality of our life. Attachments too can kill people. Radhika was much attached to Reyansh that she shared every event of her life. We all get attached to people easily but when they abandon you, it feels like we have lost a part of ourself.

Things can go horribly wrong. Not everyone can be helped by others. It was Radhika's fortune that she was helped by a generous doctor. we need to come upon any concrete decision before advancing to a conclusion and at the same time, it is also paramount to take care of those people who are associated with us. No matter how wrong our parents' outlook toward life, one thing we all need to keep in mind is that they are always at our side. They may be wrong but in that situation running away is not the solution.

Love and care can soothe everything.

Acknowledgements

To my parents who give me the strength and determination to overcome every phase of my life.

To my sister who understands me and believes in me.

To my friends who always make me happy.

To my well-wishers, my teachers who always guide me on the right path

A special thanks to my readers. This book is written for you to move in life despite every obstacles.

A special thanks to the notion press who gives me a platform to express my thought.

Wishing peace and happiness to every beautiful soul out there.

We all are angels of our own life

9 798887 494333

Printed by Libri Plureos GmbH in Hamburg, Germany